THE Forgotten CAROLS

THE Forgotten CAROLS

A Christmas Story and Songs
MICHAEL McLEAN

SHADOW MOUNTAIN
SALT LAKE CITY, UTAH

Library of Congress Cataloging-in-Publication Data
  McLean, Michael, 1952-
    The forgotten carols : a Christmas story and songs / Michael McLean.
        p.   cm.
      ISBN 1-57345-398-6 (HB)
      I. Title.
    PS3563.C3844F67   1998
    813'.54—dc21   98-8353
                                                            CIP
Printed in the United States of America

10 9   8   7   6   5   4   3   2   72082 - 6383

Contents

CHAPTER 1

My Name Is Constance

When her mother named her Constance, she had no intention of ever calling her Connie. Her mother once explained to her that Constance was a solid name, a name with substance and dignity, but "Connie," well, "Connie" was just fluff.

A lot of young girls growing up in her neighborhood would have welcomed a friendly "Hi, Connie" from their friends at school, or, at the very least, would have acknowledged the greeting with a smile. Not Constance. She corrected them resolutely. "My name is Constance," she would say, looking and sounding a bit like a stuffy old librarian with an attitude problem. "I am *not* a Connie."

She had that right. She was not then nor did she ever plan to be a "Connie."

If it is possible to be obedient to a fault, Constance was. It never occurred to her that anything her parents ever said was not absolute truth. No advice, counsel, instruction, or observation made by her parents was ever challenged. She tried in every way to be her mother in miniature. This remarkable devotion was an enormous source of pride for her parents, though Constance never knew it. All she knew was that her parents were never wrong.

That wasn't true of course. They were wrong on just about everything that had anything to do with raising healthy, well-adjusted children; they didn't teach their only child how to think or dream or feel or question or wonder or choose or discover anything for herself. They believed it was their job as parents to do all that for her—and she let them.

You'd have expected things to change when Constance turned fourteen. That was the year her parents had assured her that her mother's illness was only temporary. But that was a lie. Constance watched her mother stoically refuse to accept the truth about her condition—and the truth was, she was dying.

Typically when families receive such news, there's an initial period of denial and anger and heartbreak, followed by a sincere search for tender ways to express deep feelings and say good-bye. But Constance received only her parents' reassurance that everything was fine and that recovery was just around the corner. In fact, the only thing that even came close to resembling tenderness during that time was something Constance overheard her mother say about the nurse who helped Dr. Burton. She mentioned to her husband one evening that the nurse seemed to be a rather competent woman. It was the nearest thing to a compliment Constance had ever heard her mother give. And so it's probably no surprise that a few years after her mother's death, Constance went into nursing.

To fully appreciate what happened to Constance last Christmas, you need to know that she had been a nurse at the Fullerton Hospital her entire career. Although she could never be accused of being overly compassionate, she had never shirked her duties or failed to follow a doctor's orders to the letter. And she had never, ever questioned or challenged anyone in authority at the hospital. Needless to say, doctors loved her—and patients didn't.

It was this absolute commitment to following the voice of authority that placed Constance in an extremely awkward position a few weeks before Christmas a year ago. The chief administrator of the hospital called her into his office with a special request.

"We have . . ." (Mr. Halifax paused, wanting to say this just right) " . . . a special responsibility here at Fullerton."

Constance sat up straighter in her chair.

"This community depends on us to help them when

they need us. And to help them with the finest in hospital care requires what?"

Constance had learned in earlier private meetings with Mr. Halifax that he didn't really want her to answer these questions—that was just his way of communicating. She knew that what he really wanted was for her to act as if she had the answer on the tip of her tongue, and then he would take everything from there.

"That's right, Ms. Chamberlain; it requires money." As she expected, he answered his own question. Then he continued, "And where does this money come from? That's right, it comes from patients, or rather from insurance companies of patients. And what happens when there are difficulties collecting from these companies, Ms. Chamberlain? You were about to say that we have budget problems, and you're correct. And how do we overcome these budget shortfalls during these recessionary times? Well, we appeal to the very community we are trying to support; we give them a chance to help support us. Are you with me, Nurse Chamberlain?"

Few women would have tolerated such a patronizing

tone, but Constance was not offended. In some ways, it reminded her of dinner conversations when she was growing up, and so, strangely, she felt right at home. She nodded her agreement much as she had most of her life.

"Then you're with me. Good! We have a wonderful opportunity to participate in a goodwill public relations effort that could benefit Fullerton enormously, and I need your help."

Then something rather odd happened. Mr. Halifax became very excited, like a little boy receiving a huge gift at Christmas. She had never seen him quite like this before. Mr. Halifax went to his desk and lifted a telegram from a stack of papers.

"Listen to this!" He could hardly read it, he was so excited. "This comes from the chairman of the board of our parent company. It says, 'A prominent family has expressed interest in making a serious contribution to Fullerton in the new year. They are planning to take their holiday in Europe and will work out details of their gift when they return. They have an aging uncle whom

6

they don't feel they can take with them for various reasons—psychological more than anything, I believe— and I told them we'd be happy to have one of our outstanding nurses care for him through the holidays. This is Fullerton's opportunity to let the family know how committed we are to excellence in nursing care.'"

Mr. Halifax was almost emotional when he looked up from reading the telegram.

"Well, Nurse Chamberlain, there you have it. Straight from the chairman of the board. The schedule indicates that your wing, 3-EAST, is overstaffed this month, and, seeing as how you have no family constraints like so many others this time of year, I'd like you to handle this for me. Thank you."

He never really looked to see if she'd accepted the assignment. He simply handed her an address, a name, and a sketchy medical history. Before she could articulate a response, Mr. Halifax was shaking hands with his next appointment, and his secretary was ushering Constance out the door.

It wasn't in Constance's nature to defy the authority of

Mr. Halifax, not to mention the chairman of the board. But just because she wouldn't have said no didn't mean she would have chosen, on her own, to say yes.

The assignment she'd just been given made her feel very uncomfortable. During her nurse's training, she'd had to work in every wing in the hospital for a week or two, and the only two experiences she had found unbearable were in the psychiatric ward and the maternity ward. Years before, she had written about those weeks in her journal with uncharacteristic candor: "I can't do the babies or the crazies. It's a good thing the nursing profession offers other opportunities, or I fear I'd be forced to find another line of work."

The other thing Constance found uncomfortable was working outside the hospital itself. At Fullerton, everything was sterilized and safe. The patients would come and go, but the beds and the lamps and the furniture never changed. Although she'd read articles in trade publications about hospitals that were attracting patients with all sorts of "homey" interior decorating schemes, she was quite pleased that Fullerton remained the stark, white, antiseptic place her mother had died in. By working there, she felt like a real nurse. She wasn't certain she would be viewed as competent while nursing in someone's home.

There was some good news, however. With this assignment, she wouldn't have to be involved in all the Christmas activities that took place at the hospital. She had always thought them a nuisance—not that she was a grinch or an ogre that hated the season. But Christmas was a bit too overdone as far as she was concerned, and so this December assignment gave her the perfect escape from what she considered the clutter of the holidays. *How bad can it be?* she thought as she rode the bus home from the hospital. *I'll avoid all those people tracking snow down the halls and singing out-of-tune carols. I'll miss those silly staff parties with the gag gifts everyone pretends are so funny. And for the first time in years, I won't have to deal with the season. I'll have only one man to baby-sit during the day, and the evenings will be mine—no shift work, no nights. Maybe this is what I've always wanted: a real Christmas vacation!*

9

A faint smile came over her face as she thought about this vacation from Christmas, not realizing that she was on the eve of the most memorable Christmas she would ever know.

CHAPTER 2

A Man Forgotten

Constance checked and double-checked, but there were no convenient bus routes to the address she would be attending for the next few weeks, and inasmuch as the hospital would be covering expenses, Constance took a taxi. Since the daily routine of her life had not required her to visit this part of town before, the closer she got to her destination, the more unfamiliar everything became.

The cab driver was not a chatty soul, for which

Constance was grateful. She thought about asking him to pick her up at the end of her working day and possibly make this a routine for the next few weeks. But then it occurred to her that she might appear to be too forward, and that might encourage a familiarity she knew would make her uncomfortable—so she said nothing.

As the taxi began to slow down, her attention shifted from the new neighborhood she was entering to the fare on the meter in the cab, and she worried a bit about what kind of tip to give the driver. *Is it like tipping a waiter?* she wondered. *And if so, how does one judge the service in a taxi ride?* Since the cabby had driven safely and quietly, she decided to add 10 percent to the fare and ask for a receipt.

When she got out of the taxi and looked at the house she was about to enter, her first thought was, *So this is how the other half lives.* It was beautiful. Even though it was December, and a cold one at that, she could see that the expansive grounds around the place had been well manicured. Constance wasn't sure what size of house could rightly be called a mansion, but it occurred to her that this might be one. She walked slowly, not because she was afraid to enter, but because she was amazed that she was actually the one chosen to work here. Maybe Mr. Halifax believed she was more competent than she had ever realized.

Then something so foreign, so shocking, so bizarre happened that Constance couldn't fully comprehend it, and wouldn't for some time. She caught herself skipping toward the front door! Although she took only a few skips, it was the kind of thing a young girl with a name like Connie might have done while fantasizing that she was a princess in a magic kingdom.

Suddenly Constance became frightened. Her heart was actually pounding, and she became temporarily paralyzed on the path to the front entrance of the estate. For a few moments she trembled and shivered as if from the cold, but it wasn't that. What scared her so was the realization that for an unexplained moment she felt totally carefree, like a child at play. How could that have happened? And how could she have let it? She tried to shake off her feelings like someone who shakes off snow that collects on a winter coat during a storm, but she needed several deep breaths to regain her composure.

When she finally felt in control and competent to perform her duties, she rang the front doorbell and waited. And waited. And waited.

For a moment she felt a hint of panic. Maybe she was at the wrong address. Maybe something had gone wrong inside. Maybe . . .

From behind her came a voice that startled her.

"It's not locked. Just open the door—and if you wouldn't mind, hold it for me please."

She turned around and saw only a large, fresh-cut fir tree looking a bit like an evergreen missile rocketing toward her. She could see only the legs of whoever was propelling the tree and assumed they belonged to the voice she'd just heard. The tree showed no signs of slowing down as it approached the front door, and Constance was afraid that if she didn't open the door quickly, she might be run over. She pulled the storm door open and held it with her foot as she turned the oversized doorknob on the front door. At precisely the same moment she pushed the door open, she felt fresh Christmas-tree needles carrying her into the entry of the house.

Once inside, she maneuvered her way out of the clutches of the tree and spun free only long enough to watch the flash of green race on into another room. Like a magnet pulling her against her "when-will-I-be-properly-introduced" will, she followed the tree. When it stopped, so did she.

"Thanks! I didn't think I'd make it in without dropping it or breaking something," said the voice that had carried the tree. "Just make yourself at home and I'll be right back—got to wash the pine sap off my hands."

He disappeared into another room before the nurse got a good look at him. Now what was she supposed to do? Making herself at home wasn't something she knew how to do very well in her own place, let alone someone else's. The branches on the evergreen were still bouncing a bit from all the activity, and, though Constance didn't notice, so was she.

The room she was standing in was from another world she'd never known nor ever even dreamed of. The high, arched ceiling and paneled walls were tastefully elegant without being opulent. The furnishings were antiques so perfectly suited to the home that they didn't draw attention to how valuable they were. Where some rooms in houses that big and beautiful might intimidate their guests, this room made Constance feel, for the first time in her life, as if she were home. But after briefly indulging herself in this newfound warmth, her sense of professionalism, as she liked to think of it, caused her to dismiss her feelings.

"Hello!" said the carrier of the Christmas tree. "You must be the nurse from Fullerton Hospital. I'm sorry no one was here to properly greet you, but the butler-house-keeper-valet-and-cook was out running some errands, and I wanted so much to get the tree up today, so I went Christmas-tree shopping. It took longer than I'd planned to get this beauty, so I'm sorry I wasn't here to welcome you upon your prompt arrival. Please forgive me."

Who was this man? The nurse's mind began to race. He couldn't be the aging uncle mentioned in the telegram . . . could he? And the other family members were supposed to be off Christmasing in Europe. So who was he?

He held out his hand. "Everyone calls me Uncle John."

Constance prided herself on never staring at anyone. It wasn't polite to stare. But she was, and she couldn't help it. This must be him—her patient! But he wasn't anything like what she'd imagined. He looked so . . . so . . . so *normal*. He wasn't the old geezer with saliva trickling down the side of his mouth and hair growing out of his ears that she had dreamed about the past night. He didn't have any ticks or affectations like those she'd seen in psychiatric patients years ago. His eyes didn't have the faraway look she had prepared herself to deal with, and his clothes were beautifully coordinated and comfortably tailored. She couldn't have said why, but she had it in her mind that an older man with psychological problems would probably wear chest-high polyester plaid pants, an ugly flannel shirt, slippers, and a robe.

His hand was still extended, and finally she shook it. His grip was strong but gentle. Giving her hand a warm

17

and reassuring squeeze, he held it a bit longer than she wanted so he could guide her eyes to his when he spoke to her. "You can call me Uncle John. And what shall I call you?"

"My name is Constance . . . Constance Louise Chamberlain." As the words left her mouth, she realized she'd made a mistake. Her personal professional code demanded that she be friendly but never familiar, and here she was, right off the bat, sharing her first, last, and middle names, which she gave only when she had to on official printed material.

"Constance, eh? Well you certainly *look* like a Constance. But don't feel bad. I can see beyond that, and I believe that all people can re-create themselves if they know where to turn for help. I'll call you Connie Lou."

If real life had background music the way movies do, right then you would have heard the kind of music they play when the gunfight is about to begin. Constance's blood was running cold. He had touched a nerve, and she was straining to keep herself in check. How dare he be so critical and so familiar! After all, if anyone needed "re-creating," it would certainly be him. *He* was the patient. *He* was the one with psychological problems.

She recognized that she was losing her professional distance, so she tried to calm herself down before responding. The fact that he was still holding her hand didn't make things any easier.

"Why don't we just call me Nurse Chamberlain or Ms. Chamberlain? I'm sorry I didn't introduce myself properly in the beginning."

She was proud of herself for setting things straight so gracefully and for not losing control.

"Well, whenever 'we' call you anything, 'we'll' make sure it's either Nurse Chamberlain or Ms. Chamberlain, but as for me, I'm going to call you Connie Lou. You see, if I call you Nurse or Ms. or something equally distant and lonely, that's all you'll ever be to me. But Connie Lou . . . ah, there's someone worth getting to know."

Constance wasn't weighing her words anymore. "Sir, this isn't a date we're on here. I am a professional, and I don't believe I like the idea of a patient of mine calling me Connie Lou."

Uncle John's eyes always sparkled, but the gleam seemed to turn up a notch with each exchange in their conversation. He thought a moment and then replied, "You're right. It's not fair that I tell you what you can call me and then turn around and tell you what I'll call you."

The nurse didn't think it was visible, but her patient could see the hint of a sigh—part relief, part victory. Then, when she was confident that the matter was settled, her patient said, "You don't have to call me Uncle John just because everyone else does. Call me whatever you like. And I'll call you Connie Lou."

The background music no one could hear had changed from dueling drama to comic farce. Constance Louise Chamberlain recognized what should have been obvious before she got there: this was all a game for this man, and she couldn't take anything he said or did personally. She was dealing with someone who obviously wasn't in his right mind or else he wouldn't need a nurse to stay with him. She decided that for the good of Fullerton Hospital, and for the much-needed gift this patient's family might bring when they returned from Europe, she should play along as best she could.

"Very well then," Constance said with a smile born of inner resolve and confidence that she was handling the situation properly, "I'll call you John or Uncle John if you like. Perhaps we could sit quietly here and get better acquainted."

"That's the spirit, Connie Lou." Uncle John motioned for Constance to be seated first, and then he joined her.

"What can I tell you about me that you don't already know?" John asked while looking directly at the medical chart the nurse had created for him the night before. "Tell me something, Connie Lou. Do I look crazy to you? I mean really? Wouldn't a crazy person be wearing something like . . . like . . ." He paused a moment, not because he was deciding what he wanted to say but because he wanted to skillfully frame his words so that when he revealed them they'd achieve their full dramatic effect. " . . . like chest-high polyester plaid pants, an ugly flannel shirt, slippers, and a robe?"

There's something about someone's jaw dropping open

that's hard to disguise as anything but what it is: amazement that borders on shock. Constance could hardly believe her ears. *How did he know?* How could he *possibly* have known something she'd never told another soul in her life? She'd only thought it, and very privately at that. This was eerie . . . or it was a remarkable coincidence. Constance shook her head and decided it had to be a coincidence because the alternative was unthinkable.

"No, John, you don't look crazy to me. But then, I've never been a good judge of crazy people."

"Who has?" he responded. "The Marquis de Sade?" John couldn't help but chuckle at his own joke. He half hoped that his nurse would get it and join him, but she didn't.

The little attempt at humor hadn't warmed up Constance at all as far as John could see, so he pulled back and let her take things at her own pace. In due time, she asked John a question in a voice he recognized as the voice people use to sound professional and dignified.

"Why do you believe people think you're crazy, John?"

"Because I tell the truth," he said. "And in a world where things false and temporary are worshipped and adored, it's easier to dismiss as crazy those who tell the truth than it is to pay the price of sincerely listening to what they have to say."

He said this with no bitterness or disdain for the world his words reproached but with genuine love mingled with sadness. Although the nurse had formulated a line of questioning that would help her understand her patient's psychological imbalance, she couldn't continue along those lines—not after what she'd just heard. She wanted to know what he meant by what he said. She wanted to know why he felt the way he did. And for some reason she couldn't begin to understand, she wanted him to know that she wasn't like all those others who were shallow and superficial. She wanted him to know that and like her for it, but she didn't know if it was true. Secretly she was hoping he might be able to tell her.

Before she had a chance to ask any of the questions that were growing out of her heart instead of her head, John stood up, excused himself for a moment, and left the room. When he returned, he was carrying what looked like a very old, relatively small suitcase made from leather straps and carved wood. Constance had never seen anything else like it, and she was so preoccupied with the case itself that she didn't ask the question Uncle John was waiting for her to ask.

"Don't you want to know what's in here?" he asked with childlike enthusiasm. "These are the most precious possessions I have on earth. These are my Christmas ornaments!"

Christmas ornaments? The man's most precious possessions were the Christmas ornaments he carried around in an antique suitcase? Constance made an attitude adjustment then and there. No longer could this man be the profound poet-philosopher who would help her discover her true self. He was simply a man who probably belonged in a sanitarium.

As if he were preparing the room for someone's arrival, Uncle John went on and on about the ornaments. Each one, he claimed, had a story behind it that he told and retold every Christmas as he placed it on the tree.

As he carried on about the contents of his still-unopened suitcase, Constance had an odd thought—particularly for someone who never cared much for the folderol of putting up and taking down Christmas decorations. She thought to herself, *There can't possibly be enough ornaments in that suitcase to trim this enormous tree. Maybe he's got another box he'll bring in later.*

Strangely, Constance became so caught up in her thoughts about the ornaments and the tree that she interrupted John to ask him about the other decorations.

"Oh, this is all of them," he told her, patting the suitcase.

"Everything you need to trim this big tree is in that suitcase?" she asked incredulously.

"That's right."

"Then you *are* crazy!"

John wanted to hug her, but he was afraid she'd misunderstand, so instead he gave her his warmest smile and said, "Connie Lou, we're going to get along just fine."

Although she wasn't sure, she seemed to feel a tender,

forgotten place inside that heard him say, "You're not like all those others."

The opening of the ancient ornament case was a ritual of sorts for Uncle John. He carefully unlatched the cracked leather straps that held the case together. With each slow and deliberate motion, he seemed to be reliving a memory that was deep and sweet. As he drifted back to other places and other times, he gave life to his memories by humming something to himself. It was a melody Constance didn't recognize.

Then, as if someone had tapped him on the shoulder, he returned from his daydream, looked directly at Constance, grinned, and raised his eyebrows expectantly. Then he proudly opened the case. After quickly checking to make sure nothing was injured, he displayed his treasure for Constance to see.

When the case opened, Constance had felt something like a breath of spring enter the room. She couldn't deny it, though part of her wanted to. And she couldn't deny the little-girl anticipation she felt either. Except for her mother's death and her assignment here with John, nothing in Constance's life had ever been unexpected. Her parents were determined they would prepare her for everything. All their gifts had been practical, and therefore she knew what they would be before she opened them. All her days were scheduled, and all her activities were thoroughly planned. Even her nursing, a profession filled with the unexpected, offered her no real surprises. When she entered the field, her only real goal was competence, which for Constance meant determining in advance every action for every conceivable medical problem she might face. And her life's work meant doing just that. She even spent time on the bus to the hospital each day quietly rehearsing what she'd say during the obligatory small talk with other nurses and doctors. But she was *not* in the hospital now, and she was *not* in her parents' home now, and she was *not* caring for someone she could have prepared herself for, and so a part of her surrendered. For the first time in her life, Constance Louise Chamberlain surrendered to the simple joy of wonder.

At first glance, the only thing in John's yuletide treasure chest that reminded Constance of a Christmas ornament was the star that virtually filled the left half of the opened suitcase. The other objects were an eclectic combination of unusual, beautiful, common, foreign, and old things that all made her wonder. Where had they come from; what did they mean?

Uncle John's eyes went back and forth between his ornaments and his nurse. He would watch her eyes and guess which piece she was looking at, and then he'd quietly gaze at one with her. This went on for some time with John continuing to hum unfamiliar tunes.

"Which one goes on the tree first?" she wondered out loud.

"This one," he answered without hesitation.

He then carefully lifted from the case something that resembled an arched entrance or passageway made of stone. John placed it in the nurse's hands so she could examine it more closely.

It was fascinating. It made her think of the kind of doorways people must have entered thousands of years ago. Small as it was, it had been crafted with great attention to detail. It seemed made of real stones and mortar.

A thick piece of cloth hung where Constance expected to see a door. She asked John about it.

"Thousands of years ago, it was common to place heavy woven pieces over entrances to serve as doors," he said, sounding as though he knew what he was talking about.

Then Constance's eyes focused on something that had been painted on the stones above the entrance. It looked as though it had been written long ago in a language she could not understand.

"I made this myself," John said proudly. "It's the entrance to the inn where there was no room for Joseph and Mary. This piece always goes on the tree first."

Constance took that as her cue to place the ornament on the tree. "Where would you like me to place it?" she asked.

"We have to sing first," he answered.

Sing what? she wondered. "*O Little Town of Bethlehem*" or "*Silent Night*"? John read her thoughts.

"No, no, no, Connie Lou. Not those. We'll sing the forgotten carols."

She turned from her study of the ornament in her hand and gave John a quizzical expression. "The what?" she queried.

"The forgotten carols. That's what I call them anyway. The carols about characters who played supporting roles in the Christmas story that have either been forgotten, overlooked, misunderstood, or ignored."

"How did you find these carols?" she questioned.

"To tell you the truth, Connie Lou, they kind of found me. Take the innkeeper, for example. There was a man who turned away Joseph and Mary—not because he was mean or thoughtless. He was just taking care of business. What haunted him, though, was the feeling that he didn't really do all he could have done for the pregnant woman and her husband."

"How do you know that?" Constance asked, hoping for an answer that made sense.

"He told me," was his reply.

Sure, she thought. *That makes sense. If you're insane!*

"What do you mean, 'He told you'?" Constance felt

like getting tough. She wasn't going to get pulled into such nonsense any longer.

"He just told me. It was several years after it had happened. I had returned to Bethlehem on a sort of pilgrimage I made celebrating the birth, and I spent the night in his inn. We began talking, and the subject came up. Then, when he found out who I was, he told me his story."

"When he found out who you were? Who are you? Never mind, I don't want to know." That was certainly honest. She didn't want to know because then the spell he had cast would be broken. She wanted to cling a little longer to the hope that John was what she wanted him to be. But with everything he was telling her now, she realized he couldn't be anything other than what Mr. Halifax had said he was—an aging uncle with psychological problems.

John sat at the piano and started to play. He played well. He played with great feeling. But then, Constance never believed disturbed people were incapable of feeling—her studies had taught her that in many psychiatric cases the feelings are simply misdirected. She thought that if there was ever living proof of that, Uncle John was it.

Closing his eyes so that he would accurately reflect the spirit of the innkeeper as he remembered it, he began to sing:

> *I am a man forgotten; no one recalls my name.*
> *And thousands of years will fail to fully erase the shame.*
> *But I turned a profit nicely that day*
> *That I turned the couple away . . . I turned them away.*

His voice was hypnotic. He evoked each phrase with such a unique sense of urgency that whether you liked his voice or not, you had to listen.

> *I didn't sleep that evening, though I'd sold out my place.*
> *Somehow I felt uneasy . . . something about her face.*
> *Why did I wish that I'd let them stay?*
> *I don't think they could have paid . . . or could they have paid?*
>
> *Restless I left my bedroom.*
> *I walked the streets all night,*
> *Lost in the world I lived in.*
> *Then found by a heavenly light!*

Staring at one bright star in the sky,
I heard a baby cry.

I knew where the cry had come from
'Cause I'd told them where to go,
But I didn't think I could face them,
So sadly I slowly walked home,
Missing my chance to share in the joy.
I never saw her boy.

He never would condemn me.
I did that all on my own.
He offered His forgiveness,
And ever since then I've known
He lets us choose each hour of each day,
If we'll let Him in to stay.

Let Him in . . . let Him in . . . let the hope and joy begin.
Let Him in . . . let Him in . . . let the peace on earth
   begin.
Whether it be in your world today
Or a crowded Bethlehem inn,
Find a way . . . make Him room . . . let Him in.

When the singing of the first forgotten carol was over,
Uncle John rose from the piano, took Constance by the
hand, and walked over to the bare Christmas tree. He

pointed to the spot on the tree that he found worthy of this ornament. He called the spot the "heart of the tree." Constance hung the ornament far enough in on the ever-green branch that there was no danger of it accidentally falling off. And as she did, she noticed again the strange writing across the top of the ornament. John read her thoughts and answered, "That was the inscription writ-ten by the innkeeper over the entrance to his inn shortly before he died. I wanted to preserve it on the ornament just the way my friend had written it. It says: 'Let Him In.'"

Before excusing himself to take a nap, Uncle John showed Constance around the main floor of the house. He wanted her to be comfortable, though he knew such a thing was difficult for her. He explained that the butler, who while the family was away also served as the house-keeper, valet, and cook, would be working around the house and that she should not be alarmed when she heard him come in the back way. Uncle John also men-tioned that the butler was shy and probably wouldn't say much, but that she would be a fool to pass up his egg salad sandwiches on rye, were he to offer her some.

Uncle John reminded her that she was free to leave at five o'clock and asked her not to wake him to say good-bye. He also requested that she leave her phone number on the pad by the telephone in the hall so the butler could call her in an emergency. Then he climbed the long staircase and was gone.

The rest of the afternoon passed rather uneventfully. She heard the butler come in, but the only glimpse she caught of him was when she went into the kitchen to get a drink of water. From what she could tell, which wasn't much, he was about the same size as Uncle John, with a bit of a belly, a full beard, and very thick glasses.

At the stroke of five, she called a cab and prepared to go home. Although she'd never given out her home phone number to a man of any age, she felt relatively safe in leaving her number on the pad by the phone as she'd been asked. Her patient was obviously suffering from bouts of delusion, but if today proved anything, it was that he was perfectly harmless.

CHAPTER 3

Homeless

About ten minutes past five o'clock, the cab arrived. When Constance told the driver her address, he surprised her by asking which route she preferred, "E" Street or Charleston Avenue. She didn't want him to know how unfamiliar she was with the area, but her long hesitation gave her away. Trying to disguise her indecision, she suggested he take the route with the least rush-hour traffic.

Five minutes later, the knot Constance usually felt in her stomach when she was in unfamiliar territory started to tighten. She was in the heart of the homeless section of town when the traffic slowed to a snail's pace. Ahead she could see the flashing lights of an ambulance and a police car.

Instinctively the nurse told the cab driver to pull over to the side of the road and wait for her. As a professional nurse, she felt it her duty to offer assistance at the scene of an accident. As she approached the flashing lights, she took a few deep breaths and introduced herself to the nearest police officer.

"Excuse me. I'm a nurse at Fullerton Hospital. Can I be of any assistance?"

"Thank you for offering, but it looks like the paramedics have things under control."

"What happened?"

"A minor accident. They think the driver may have broken his collarbone, but that's about all. Fortunately no one else was hurt. Excuse me." The officer then began clearing the crowd and trying to direct traffic around the accident.

On the walk back to the taxi, Constance noticed the mattresses on the streets and the cardboard shelters leaned against the side of old buildings. *People actually live here,* she thought, and she wondered how many of them were sick or would soon become sick in such conditions.

Although she'd seen homeless people at the hospital before and had treated several, it was different walking among them. She felt a compassion that was absent in her hospital work as she walked along the street where these people tried to survive.

As she crossed the last side street before reaching her taxi, she heard some street singing. A group was huddled around a fire they had built in an old metal garbage can spray painted like a Christmas tree. They sang a bittersweet Christmas song that Constance had never heard before:

> *Homeless, homeless,*
> *Like the Christ child was . . . we are*
> *Homeless, homeless,*
> *But there is hope because*

39

He came down to earth to lead us,
And He vowed He'd never leave us
Homeless, homeless,
For in His love there is a home.

The song had captured her attention, but the singing of it, with such hope and optimism, was capturing her heart.

Homeless, homeless,
Was His humble birth.
Homeless, homeless,
And still He changed the earth.
Nothing kept His heart from giving
Though most of His life was living
Homeless, homeless.
He showed it's how we live,
Not where.
And when His homeless days on earth were done,
He went home to where we all came from.
And He went to prepare
A mansion for us there.
He gave His whole life to lead us,
And I know He'll never leave us

Homeless, homeless,
For in His love there is a home.

As she pulled herself away from this unlikely group of Christmas carolers, she was struck by how much she wanted to give them something—some money, a handout—but no one asked. Here, of all places, she would have expected panhandlers and beggars, but instead she found dignity and hope. Where had it come from, she wondered as the taxi drove her home. Where had it come from?

After supper and before calling it a day, she thought she'd read awhile. She tried to get into her routine of studying from nursing journals and medical books, but for some reason, that was impossible. Then she tried to do some casual reading, but nothing she read was anywhere near as interesting as her own reflections on the day. Later, while she was getting ready for bed, she detected that sense of anticipation she'd felt earlier that day. But she didn't fight it. And while she brushed out her hair, she found herself humming tunes that until today she'd never heard before.

CHAPTER 4

You Were Not There in Bethlehem

*T*he next day at the mansion, Constance was greeted at the door by the butler. *Greeted* is probably the wrong word; he didn't say anything to her that she could properly understand. After opening the door for her, he mumbled something and went upstairs. *He must be going to announce my arrival to Uncle John*, she thought.

She hung her coat and scarf up in the hall closet and

found a comfortable chair in the main room and waited. Then she heard a clear, thin sound coming from upstairs. It sounded like a wooden flute of some kind. The melody was hypnotic, but the actual sound of the instrument was even more so.

As the sound got closer, she expected any moment to see Uncle John coming down the stairs playing whatever instrument was making that remarkable sound. What she didn't expect to see was a man dressed like a shepherd who lived at the time of Christ. But that's how John looked.

The clothes he was wearing were as remarkable as the sound he'd been making. To say that he looked as though he'd just walked out of the movie *Ben Hur* would be an insult, really, because he looked more authentic than anything ever portrayed in a movie. His entrance was so convincing that for a moment Constance didn't think he just *looked* like a shepherd from Judea's plains, but she thought he *was* one.

But reality soon came into focus for the professional nurse. And when it did, she didn't know whether to be concerned for her patient's behavior or amused by it. Contrary to her nature, she chose the latter.

As he played his haunting tune, he circled his nurse a few times and then motioned her to follow him, Pied-Piper style. She did, and he guided her to the opened case of Christmas ornaments. Continuing to play the music, he nodded his head toward the ornaments, hoping that Constance would read his thoughts. Strangely enough, she did.

She saw a beautiful miniature shepherd's flute like the one John was playing, and she picked it up. It was a remarkable likeness, with tiny wooden reeds cut and shaped to look like an ancient instrument. John continued to play for her while she examined the ornament, and then he marched her toward the Christmas tree. Not wanting to stop playing so he could speak, he used his eyes and head movement to give her the message that she was to place the little flute on the tree.

Constance thought she was playing along beautifully and began to hang the ornament on the tree when suddenly John's flute-playing sounded like a swarming hive of angry bees. Constance felt a surge of panic and almost dropped the little flute. *What was wrong? What was happening? Was he having a seizure? What should she do?*

The state of emergency she was preparing in her mind to handle didn't last long, however. John took the flute away from his lips long enough to say, "Don't put it so close to the other one, Connie Lou. It's a big tree." When he could see that Constance knew what he meant, he went on playing.

Constance decided to hold the miniature flute in a general area of the tree and see if the location met with the shepherd's approval before committing herself to hanging the ornament. She first held it in a space due south of the only other ornament on the tree, and then she looked to John. He gave her a "so-so" back-and-forth nod and played a mediocre note over and over again. She decided to try another spot much higher and to the right. Victory! The music soared, and she knew she'd found the spot. As she hung the little flute, her back was to John so he didn't see her smile from its beginning, but as she turned around he caught the last piece of it, and it was beautiful.

When the musical phrase he was playing came to a natural pause, he started to sing.

> *The flock was more than peaceful.*
> *The night was dark and deep.*
> *The stillness wrapped around me,*
> *And I drifted off to sleep.*
> *And when my friends awoke me,*
> *Oh, what a tale they had to tell!*

Between verses he played his flute.

> *They said the angels told them*
> *About the new-born king.*
> *They had a star to guide them.*
> *They heard the heavens sing.*
> *They said that when they found Him,*
> *They knew they'd never be the same.*

Again he played an interlude before singing the carol's first chorus.

> *Somehow I did believe them*
> *Though everything I knew said I should not believe them.*
> *This story can't be true.*

> *But there was something magic in the air*
> *That made me feel as if I had been there.*

The rhythm of the song, the theme, everything about it was different from anything Constance thought of as "Christmas music," but it was doing the very thing her past Christmases had failed to do—it was moving her heart.

> *I asked a thousand questions.*
> *Their answers startled me.*
> *The more I heard, the more I thought*
> *I knew this could not be.*
> *And then the struggle started—*
> *My head was wrestling with my heart.*
> *Why would a God from heaven*
> *Come to the world this way?*
> *Why in a lowly stable*
> *Would the Messiah lay?*
> *I shook my head and asked them*
> *To tell the story one more time.*

> *And, yes, I did believe them*
> *Though I'd not seen a thing.*
> *I did not go to Bethlehem*
> *Or hear the angels sing,*

But there was something magic in the air
That made me feel as if I had been there.
I knew that as the world
Moves on through time,
There would be more stories just like mine
About the souls who've chosen to believe
In something that they never got to see.

And do you think you'll join us
Though you've not seen a thing?
You were not there in Bethlehem
Nor heard the angels sing.
But if you feel the spirit in the air,
Then, just like me, you'll know that
He was here . . . He was here.
The King of kings and Lord of lords was here,
He was here . . . He was here.
And He will come again, for He was here.

As John repeated the chorus, he became more and more emotional. It was as if he had to make sure Constance knew what he knew.

Constance had seen evangelical preachers on television before and always felt uncomfortable when they became emotional. She thought their crying was simply an act—staged to get more money. But what she was feeling at that moment with John was completely different. As a nurse, she had seen men cry from pain, but in her whole life she'd never been around a man who cried the sweet tears of spiritual gratitude and joy. She felt something welling up inside, and she knew she had to push it back where it came from. First of all, she had never cried in front of anyone, and she couldn't let that happen now—not in front of a patient. But her greater concern was that she didn't know what it was that she was feeling.

Perhaps it was the magic in the air.

Uncle John took Constance's hand and walked her over to the sofa, where he sat her down.

"Thank you," he said gratefully, "for letting me share that with you. I love that shepherd."

Sitting next to John gave her a chance to feel the fabric of his costume against her skin. "Where did you get this material?" she asked. "I've never seen anything else like it."

"This was his, actually. He told me that he wanted me

to have it so I'd never forget his story. I never have, and on the day I place his ornament on the tree, I wear his clothes to honor him."

Constance wondered what had happened to Uncle John in his life to make him need to create these fantasies. Even though she was not skilled in clinical psychology, she tried to remember her courses on the subject back in college. She dared to ask a few questions in hopes they would help her get a clearer picture of his mental illness. "Your friend, this . . . this shepherd. He died when?" she asked.

"About A.D. 42, I believe," he said, straining to remember.

"But you've lived all this time since then. Is that right?"

"That's right."

"Don't you think that's a little unusual?" she probed.

"A *little?* It's absolutely *incredible!* How many people do you know who have been around as long as I have?"

His response to her question surprised her.

"How long do you think you've been around, John?"

"Oh, it's getting close to two thousand years." After a moment he nodded to himself that his estimate was correct and then continued. "I'd say that's more than a little unusual, wouldn't you, Connie Lou?"

"I'd say it's unbelievable."

"Well, of course it's unbelievable. If it hadn't happened to me, I'd have a hard time believing it myself."

"How did it happen that you have been alive all this time?"

John's expression grew a bit more serious. Constance thought she might have hit a nerve, and so she watched him carefully. She had learned in her psychology studies that body language can be very telling.

"I can't tell you," he finally said.

"You can't tell me because you don't want to or because you don't really know how it happened?" Constance felt very good about her question.

"You wouldn't understand—not now, anyway—so let's just leave it at that." John stood up. Constance immediately recognized his standing as the body-language clue she had been looking for. John was obviously uncomfortable talking about this and wanted to escape, but she wasn't about to let him.

"What are you running away from, John?"

He looked puzzled at her question. Constance took his look as more evidence that she was on to something. She persisted.

"What are you running away from?"

"I'm not running away from anything."

"Oh yes you are," she proclaimed.

"No I'm *not!*" he fired back.

"Then why did you stand up just now?" she said slyly.

"*Because old shepherd clothes itch!* I'm going to change." He walked out of the room, leaving his psychologist to read that body language any way she wanted.

CHAPTER 5

A Voice That
Cannot Sing

Constance decided that she would have to back off for a while. She'd find ways to get to the root of his psychosis if she were patient, she believed. She'd become his friend . . . an ally . . . and then when he was safe with her, he'd share the innermost feelings of his soul, and she would bring him triumphantly out of the world of his delusions into the world of reality.

She was imagining what that would be like—to change someone's life. How proud her parents would have to be of her, if they were alive. How proud she would feel of herself! She lingered on these feelings for quite a while.

Then, awkwardly crashing through the swinging door that led to the kitchen, came the butler with a silver tray full of food and two glasses of juice. He practically dropped the tray on the coffee table near the sofa where she sat, and, as he walked back toward the kitchen, she heard him mumble, "Egg salad on rye."

The sandwiches did look good, and John had told her she'd be foolish to pass them up, but she didn't know whether to wait for John or to go ahead. While she was trying to decide what to do, she heard Uncle John's voice come from upstairs.

"Are those egg salad sandwiches on rye I smell? Connie Lou, you go ahead and get started. I'll be right down."

Constance took one of the half sandwiches and sniffed it before taking a bite. She'd never noticed egg salad to

56

have much of a smell at all. John must be very sensitive to aromas, she thought, and then she took a bite. Ambrosia! Uncle John was right. Anyone who passed these up was a fool.

Uncle John joined her, dressed as he had been the day before, and he looked comfortable. As they ate, they both commented on what a treat the food was, and when they finished, Uncle John announced, "Time we do another ornament."

From his special case of Christmas ornaments he selected one that looked like a very old writing tool. When John presented it to Constance for her inspection, she could still see the ink stains on the tip.

When she handed the pen back to John, he walked it over to the tree and was about to place it there with the other two ornaments when something shocked Constance. A thought seized her brain and made her captive to its wishes. She quietly raced to the piano and began pounding on the keys with reckless abandon. When Uncle John's head spun around to see what was the matter, she saw in his eyes the kind of bewildered panic she'd experienced herself not long ago. When she had his complete attention, with grand dramatic effect she said, "Don't put it so close to the other one, Uncle John. It's a *big* tree!"

Her laughter started as a mischievous little chuckle that emanated from her brain. Then it swept through her body like a fire that hit full strength in her stomach, and before she could contain it, she was laughing uncontrollably. It was contagious. John began laughing a bit himself at the joke she had played on him, but it grew to his own belly laugh simply because his nurse was laughing so crazily. She tried so hard to stop, but just when she thought she had herself under control, another wave of laughter would overcome her. Tears came to her eyes, and her sides ached. It was as if all the laughter of a lifetime was being released in one afternoon.

She had not planned it, rehearsed it, or even thought about it. It just happened, and it marked her second great surrender in as many days—to the innocent joy of laughter.

When the laughter finally died down, Constance

braced herself for the embarrassment she expected. But it never came. Maybe it was the environment, maybe it was the season, maybe it was her patient who made her feel safe somehow. She didn't know why, but she felt that an enormous weight had been lifted from her shoulders, and she was renewed.

Uncle John still had the pen in his hand, and he took it with him to the piano. He placed it as a source of inspiration on the piano's music stand and then began to play. The music would underscore the story he was about to tell.

"Connie Lou, I want to tell you about this pen. I received it from a man who told me his story late one evening many Christmases ago.

"We were talking about inspiration—where it comes from, why it comes, how it changes us. And he spoke of a time when he felt completely uninspired, without direction, lost. And then he had a dream.

"'In my dream,' he told me, 'I was a very young angel in a very heavenly place when a trumpet was sounded and an announcement made. All the angels were invited to audition for the choir that would announce the Holy Birth. The excitement and anticipation caused my little angel heart almost to burst.

"'When my moment arrived, I stood before the musical tribunal and sang . . . and sang . . . and sang. No one interrupted or snickered at me because, well, this was heaven. But I knew immediately that I would not be invited to join the choir for one obvious reason: I couldn't sing. I felt the music, but I couldn't get that feeling to come into my voice.

"'The Grand Chorus Master smiled and nodded to his chief assistant to show me out. "This isn't fair," I pleaded. "If you could hear what is in my heart, you'd let me sing." I ran back toward the Chorus Master and begged him to give me another chance. And as I did, music began to fill the room. And I recognized it, for it was the music coming directly from my tender, innocent heart.'"

As John played the young angel's forgotten carol, Constance heard instruments from an orchestra—faint at first, then loud enough to be in the room with them. And then she heard a choir singing glorious alleluias. How could that be? Where was the sound coming from? Was her patient's psychosis contagious? Had she been seduced into his delusions?

She had nowhere to turn for answers, and so she surrendered to the music, and it filled her in ways the answers she was seeking never could.

Then, with full orchestral underscore, John completed his story: "'All the other angels stood motionless and amazed as they heard the sound, and when my carol to my King was over, the Grand Chorus Master stood.

"'"Oh little one," he said, "you have so much to give, and your time will come."

"'"Then I can't sing with the choir?" I looked for him to change his mind, but he only shook his head and smiled.

"'"You have a different voice, but it *will* be heard. Centuries from now it will be heard. More orchestras and choirs than you can now imagine will be giving the music of your heart a voice that will echo through time."'"

As John played the final strains of this forgotten carol's melody, Constance heard a descant from the unseen orchestra. She recognized the countermelody as "Joy to the World," which turned into the "Halleluia Chorus" and ended as the finale from "For unto Us a Child Is Born."

"It was *Handel?*" Constance exclaimed. "This is the pen of George Frideric Handel?"

"The one he wrote the *Messiah* with," John clarified.

"I can't believe it," she said.

"No," John corrected her, "you won't believe it. There's a big difference."

"What do you mean?" she said a little defensively.

"You made up your mind a long time ago that something like this could never happen, and so you've chosen not to believe it could be true."

"But it doesn't make any sense," Constance argued.

"Why doesn't it?" he asked.

"Because things like that just don't happen." She was getting angry.

"Says who?"

"Says my mother!" She couldn't stop the words from racing out of her mouth. And when she said them, she sounded just like the schoolgirl she once was. She knew that John could have made a field day out of a response like that. She was waiting for him to tease her the way the children at school used to do. But instead of attacking, he retreated.

"Connie Lou, I'm sorry. You don't have to believe me. There's nothing wrong with you because you can't believe me. The most natural thing in the world is to question things and want to know why. You haven't failed. You haven't done anything wrong. You're my friend, and I apologize for sounding like I was judging you. Please forgive me."

No one had ever asked for Constance's forgiveness before, so she wasn't sure how to give it. And no one had ever told her before that she was all right. People had told her she was competent, but until this moment, she'd never been told that as she was, she was all right. She'd never been told it was fine to feel and question and challenge and disagree with an adult. She'd never been treated like this before, and so she didn't know how to act.

Uncle John then took the pen that he claimed once belonged to Handel, and he dipped it into a little ink bottle that was in the ornament case. He then wrote something on a piece of paper, blew the fresh ink dry, and handed the paper to Constance. Before she could read it, he told her it was time for his nap, and he left the room.

His note read:

> Connie Lou, I'm afraid you're stuck with me, and I hope you will learn to like me someday, because you can't make me not like you.
>
> John

Constance held the note written with the same pen that supposedly wrote the glorious music of Handel's *Messiah*. She still couldn't believe it had, but she could believe one thing: today it had written something beautiful.

CHAPTER 6

Mary Let Me Hold Her Baby

It started snowing that afternoon, and Constance found herself drawn to the overstuffed chair by the window so she could watch. Although she had a great deal on her mind, the falling snow gave her an excuse to think about nothing for a while. It was a soft and gentle snow, the kind that brings quiet. As she sank into the deep, goose-down cushions of her chair, she gazed out the window and watched the ground become a thick, white carpet. The butler bumbled into the room and lit a fire in the fireplace, but she barely noticed. The world became soft and peaceful and safe and warm, and she hoped nothing would disturb her for a while.

Through the lace curtain of falling snow, she saw some children starting to build a snowman. Among them was an older woman who looked as if she was having as much fun as the children were. Constance was amazed that a woman that old could be so childlike, so carefree, so . . . so much fun. Constance wondered if the woman was the children's grandmother.

"What a wonderful surprise. It's Sarah!" Had John not spoken, Constance would not have noticed that he had entered the room. He tapped on the window and tried to get the attention of the woman playing in the snow with the children.

"Oh, Connie Lou, you have to meet her," he said enthusiastically. Then he opened the window and called, "Sarah! Sarah! Come in out of the cold."

The old woman was helping the children place the head on the snowman. "In a minute, John, in a minute."

"You're going to adore this woman, Connie Lou," Uncle John said confidently. "Everybody does. She's one of my favorite forgotten carols."

"She's *what?*" Constance said as she sat up on the edge of her chair. Uncle John's carol did some of the explaining:

> *She had a way with children,*
> *And she molded them like clay.*
> *She found the greatness in them,*
> *And she nurtured it each day.*
> *Though she never had been married*
> *Or had children of her own,*
> *She could help the toughest child be good.*
> *And so she would not be misunderstood,*
> *She told her story every chance she could.*

Uncle John greeted Sarah at the door with a warm embrace, and he walked her to the fire.

"Connie Lou, this is my dear friend Sarah. Sarah, this is my new friend Connie Lou Chamberlain."

Constance stood and went over to shake hands. "My

name is Constance. I'm really not a Connie," she said out of habit. "How long have you and John been friends?"

"Forever," Sarah answered, and then she smiled at John. "Well, not exactly forever. It just seems that long. What's it really been, John? About nineteen hundred years?"

Constance shrieked inside, *Oh, no! She's crazy too!* But after a few seconds, she managed to calm herself down so she could ask a few more questions.

"What brings you to this part of . . . of . . . the planet?" Constance didn't know what else to say.

"I try to look up John every few hundred years to see if he still remembers me—and if he remembers my carol."

John smiled at his old friend. "I remember, Sarah. I always remember." Then something very curious happened. John went to his ornament case and pulled out something Constance had no idea was there: a large, soft square of cloth. "Swaddling clothes," he said. And when he handed them to Sarah, she held them as if she were holding a baby. Then she sang sweetly and quietly, as if she were singing a lullaby:

Mary let me hold her baby,
Her newborn son.
Though I'd never be a mother,
I felt like one.
Mary let me hold her baby
So she could rest.
Ever since that night I held Him,
My life's been blessed.

Sarah hummed quietly and rocked the imagined baby in her arms. As she did, John whispered to Constance, "She single-handedly built the largest orphanage in ancient Israel and served there for years. I tried to help her whenever I could."

Constance marveled. "And she never had children of her own?" she asked.

"No one could convince her of that. Every child she met, she loved as her own until the day she died."

"She died? You're telling me this woman's dead?" Constance was whispering too.

"She's just a spirit," John said, keeping his voice low, "but she's doing great work on the other side, I'm told."

"The other side?"

"Of the veil. Sometimes it's very thin, Connie. Sometimes it's very thin."

Sarah sang the final verses of her forgotten carol while rocking the baby she still saw in her arms.

> *Those like me who can't have children*
> *Still can be mothers.*
> *Something in His eyes convinced me*
> *I could serve so many others.*
> *Mary let me hold her baby*
> *So soft and warm.*
> *Mary let me hold her baby,*
> *And I was reborn.*

"Shhh, he's asleep," Sarah said. Then she walked over to Constance. "You hold him for a while so I can visit with John." Then she placed the swaddling clothes in the nurse's arms and walked into the other room with the old man.

At first Constance thought she would feel silly holding the blanket in the room all alone. But she didn't. Instead, her heart swelled with so much love that she thought it would burst. And for a moment, just a moment, she thought she saw a baby looking up at her from within the swaddling clothes. Without realizing what she was doing, she started to hum Sarah's lullaby . . .

Then a snowball hit the window, and she awoke. Disoriented, she looked around but saw no one. *I must have dozed off for a few minutes*, she thought. She checked the clock—the time was half past five. She'd been asleep nearly two hours. How embarrassing! How unprofessional!

She hurried to get her things and then called a cab. While she was waiting for it to arrive, something on the Christmas tree caught her eye—an ornament she hadn't seen before. It was a cloth bow made from a fragment of swaddling clothes.

CHAPTER 7

A Music Box and an Old Corsage

Halfway home, Constance realized that in her rush to leave, she'd forgotten her notebook. She probably could have waited to pick it up the next day, but since the hospital was paying the cab fare, she asked the driver to turn around and take her back to the mansion.

When she got to the front door, she decided not to knock but simply to slip inside. *No need to bother anyone,* she thought. *The butler won't mind, and John's probably asleep anyway.*

She quietly opened the door and tiptoed in. Then she saw Uncle John dancing around the Christmas tree. The music came from a small music box, and the tinkling sound reminded her of something from a Christmas ballet, but it wasn't a tune she recognized. It had almost a bittersweet quality to it.

Constance stayed out of view and watched John dance for a few moments. He had no partner, of course, but his every gesture, his every glance, made it clear that whoever he was remembering was someone very special.

When the music box went silent, he bowed to his partner, kissed her hand, and took her by the arm to the ornament case. From it he took what looked like a corsage of dried flowers. Then, pantomiming, he pinned it on her. After that, John and his imaginary partner danced their way around the room toward the tree. If they were dancing to music, only they could hear it.

During one of his turns, John saw that he was being watched, and it broke the spell. He just stood there looking at Constance, sad but not angry that the magic of the memory had faded. Constance was about to explain why she had come back and why she entered without knocking, but John spoke first.

"She was my only true love. I have lived long enough to say honestly that I have seen the great beauties of the world, but she was the greatest. Her eyes were windows to a stunningly beautiful soul . . . and she loved me. She saw things in me I couldn't see myself and found a way to bring them out. Over the centuries I have listened as the world's finest composers have tried to capture in music the very essence of true love. For other loves they may have succeeded, but for our love, no melody on earth has come close."

He stared at the corsage of dried flowers in his hand, then went on: "In all these years, the only time I really wished I could die was when she did. Only two things kept me going. One was the fact that she made me promise I'd finish my mission—with honor, no matter what. The other was the hope that we will be together forever someday.

"I do pretty well the rest of the year. But when I dance our Christmas dance and place her corsage on the tree, I miss her."

There was a loud honk. The cab driver was still waiting. Constance had to go, but with all her heart she wished she could stay with the old man so he wouldn't be alone. Constance never thought of herself as the kind of woman men would find attractive, but she wanted to do something for John—dear, confused John. So she signalled the taxi to wait and then walked over to the music box and wound it up. When it began to play, she stood before her patient and asked, "May I have this dance?"

He pinned the corsage on her crisp white uniform, bowed, took her right hand in his left, and placed his right hand in the small of her back. And then they danced.

It should have been more difficult for Constance than it was. She didn't know how to dance. She could barely remember the last time she had danced, and what a disaster it had been. But this dance wasn't for her—it was for him. She'd been a prisoner to her own concerns, her own insecurities, and her own problems most of her life. But tonight, in the arms of a lonely old man, love was setting her free. Not romantic love. But some kind of love. She'd had so little experience with love in her life that she didn't know what to call it. But the man she was dancing with knew exactly what kind of love it was— pure.

When their dance was over, she unpinned the corsage and placed it on the tree, and then, as she was leaving, she kissed Uncle John on the cheek.

As she rode home, she wasn't filled with anxieties about what she'd just done. Even though she'd danced with a patient and kissed him, she didn't feel the slightest guilt or awkwardness or concern. She was at peace. Totally at peace.

As the taxi drove through town, she saw a Christmas banner proclaiming: "PEACE ON EARTH." For the first time in her life, she knew what that meant.

CHAPTER 8

A Heart That Cannot Hear

*W*hen Constance had finished her dinner and washed the dishes, she sat in her favorite reading chair and just looked around the room. *This room needs something,* she thought. Then she said half aloud, "Maybe I should go out and get a small Christmas tree. It looks kind of drab in here."

When the words left her mouth, the furniture she'd

lived with for so long seemed to cry out in protest. *What are you saying?* the room seemed to ask. *This is what you are. You can't change it! What are you thinking? You can't put up a little tree and disguise who you are. You can't leave the tree up all year round. Constance, don't get caught up in your patient's insanity. Be professional. Be competent!*

With this, her peace vanished. Suddenly she felt a knot in her stomach. What had she done? She'd gone against her better judgment. She'd allowed a patient to seduce her into his psychosis. She'd lost her professional distance. She'd compromised her professional standards. She had failed, and she felt sick. Now what was she going to do? She'd have to tell Mr. Halifax. How humiliating! What would he think? What would become of her? She could lose her job, her world. No, she wouldn't tell anyone, but she'd ask for Mr. Halifax to replace her immediately, and she'd fill in for whatever nurse he chose. She'd do it in the morning. First thing. *There now. Take a few deep breaths*, she told herself. *That's better. Everything's going to be all right.*

But Constance didn't sleep. Instead, she rehearsed

what she would say to Mr. Halifax. She went over and over what he'd say and then how she'd respond. As long and difficult as the night was, there was something familiar about it. It was a bit extreme, perhaps, but the nurse reasoned that this might be what it took to bring her back to her senses.

First thing the next morning, she started calling Mr. Halifax, who was always at the office at seven o'clock sharp. But he was already in a meeting. She left both her home number and the phone number at the mansion and pleaded with his secretary to have him return the call as quickly as possible. Between seven o'clock and the time she had to leave to fulfill her duties, she left five messages. She received no call.

As she rode in the cab, she thought things would be much easier if she were in an accident. Everyone would understand then. She wouldn't have to face Uncle John again, and she wouldn't have to explain to Mr. Halifax why she wanted to be released from her responsibilities. She'd be safely cared for in the hospital she knew so well with its stark, white, antiseptic walls.

There was no accident, however. She arrived at the home of Uncle John without incident, and precisely on time. She paid the cab driver and walked slowly to the door. There was no skipping, no dancing, no childlike excitement. She was painfully aware of who she was and why she was there.

Reluctantly she rang the front doorbell, and Uncle John opened the door for her.

"Good morning," he said cheerfully. "Sleep well?"

Constance didn't answer.

"You just missed a call from your boss," John informed her. "He said he'd be in meetings most of the day but that he'd try to call you when he had his next break." John seemed to sense that something was wrong. "Connie Lou, are you feeling all right?" he asked with genuine concern.

"I've been better," was all she could say.

"Well then, I've got just the thing." John was beaming. "I have an old herbal tea remedy that works every time. I'll have some made up for you right away."

"Please don't bother. I'll be fine." Constance knew

that her performance was unconvincing, but it was the best she could do under the circumstances.

"You're worried about something, Connie Lou. It's written all over your face. What is it?"

"It's nothing."

"Is it about last night? Are you feeling funny about last night?"

How does he always know everything, she wondered. *Can psychotics read minds?*

"Connie Lou, may I tell you something? That was one of the dearest things anyone has ever done for me, and I appreciate you so much. Come here, I want to show you something." He walked her over to the Christmas tree, then waited for her to discover his surprise. Because she didn't know what she was supposed to be looking for, it took her a minute to recognize what Uncle John wanted her to see—the newest ornament on the tree, a red cross.

"I made this last night, after you left. You know I met Florence Nightingale—served with her, in fact, for a few months."

Constance rolled her eyes. Didn't he *ever* give up?

"But last night," Uncle John continued, "you showed this patient of yours compassion that matched anything I ever saw Florence do. So in your honor I made this red cross and placed it on the tree."

Constance noticed that the ornament was placed very near the corsage.

"So what's the song that goes with it?" she asked almost sarcastically.

"Only you can write that one, Connie Lou," he answered.

"But I don't write songs."

"Oh yes you do," Uncle John said. "We all do. It's just harder for some of us to let them out, that's all."

"Let them out?"

"Out of our hearts," he said. "We may not all be George Frideric Handel, but every meaningful experience we ever have has a song that accompanies it. And we write it in our hearts. Our favorite songs that other people write are the ones that come closest to sounding like the ones we have inside us. And you're writing the one that goes with this ornament right now."

"I'm writing a song . . . right now?" Constance already knew the man was crazy, but he was really proving it now.

"Not consciously, of course. It's all happening inside. And when you're willing to let it be heard, it will."

Constance just looked at her patient for a long time. She had no words. She was searching for some, but none came. *How do you reason with someone who's lost all touch with reality?* she wondered. *And more important, why am I trying?* He was beyond hope, as far as she could see. He showed no willingness to acknowledge the fact that he was living in a fantasy world. And she realized this was beginning to bother her.

"Why do you do this?" she asked.

"Do what?"

"Make up all those stories about how long you've lived and the people you've known and how everybody writes songs in their hearts. It's not normal. It's strange. It's not reality. It's not true—"

She had more to say, but Uncle John interrupted her. "Wait a minute. What I've told you may be strange, I grant you that, and it may not be normal or seem real to you, but, as I told you before, I tell the truth."

"Well, I guess all truth is relative," she acknowledged.

John got a bit stern with her for a moment. "Listen, Connie Lou, just because you don't understand something doesn't mean it can't be true. I can respect the fact that you don't believe what I've been telling you, but that doesn't mean it isn't so. The problem with a lot of people who've only been around a few decades is that they cling so tightly to the things they learned yesterday that they can't reach out for the new things that will change their tomorrows."

Uncle John paused. He knew it would take a moment for what he'd said to sink in, and he wanted Constance to think about it before he continued. She did. And then she asked, "But how can you know if something's true when it flies in the face of everything else you think you've learned?"

"That's why we have hearts, Connie Lou. If we'll let them, they are our true teachers. We just have to listen."

"To our *hearts?*" she asked thoughtfully.

86

"That's right—to our hearts." John pointed to the Christmas tree to help make his point. "This season is a perfect example of what I'm talking about. How could anyone believe the story of Christmas, and of a Savior coming to save us, born of a virgin, were it not for a willingness to listen to our hearts? I met a woman a lot like you who learned this for herself one evening when she happened to see Joseph and thought she recognized him. I know because I happened to be visiting him at the time."

John began to sing:

> *He was working late one evening*
> *With the wood he knew so well,*
> *When she thought she recognized him,*
> *Though at first she couldn't tell.*
> *As she humbly begged his pardon,*
> *A strange sadness swelled inside*
> *When she asked, "Aren't you the father*
> *Of the man they crucified?"*
> *Then the carpenter repeated*
> *What he'd said so many times.*
> *He said, "I was not His father; He was mine."*
> *Then he humbly went on working*
> *With his worn and calloused hands.*

Though she did not ask more questions,
He knew she did not understand.
And so he asked if she would help him.
He saw her answer in a glance.
And then she did the chores he asked her,
And she felt grateful for the chance.
And then he talked for hours of Jesus,
And how he knew He was divine.
He said, "I was not His father; He was mine.
How could one so foolish and so flawed
Ever hope to raise the Son of God?"
Then he spoke of the misgivings
He had had a thousand times,
And how Jesus found the tender moments
To let him know he'd done just fine.
Then the carpenter recited
The greatest truths he'd ever learned
And testified they came from Jesus.
And then her heart within her burned.
They embraced as she departed,
And Joseph told her one more time,
"Tell them I was not His father;
Tell them He was mine. No, I was
Not His father; He was mine."

John took from his ornament case a small replica of a cradle, which he told Constance looked very much like the one Joseph had built for Jesus. Then he respectfully hung it on the tree and turned to Constance.

"In all my years on earth, I have seen time and time again that those who are happiest are those who have the courage to follow their hearts—to believe what otherwise would be unbelievable; to seek the light; to find the truth . . ."

Music entered the room. It was a presence that was very discernible and very real:

> *Somewhere beneath the glitter*
> *That comes this time of winter,*
> *In many souls there is a cry.*
> *They may not clearly say it,*
> *But in their hearts they pray it.*
> *And you can see it in their eyes.*

Constance heard a choir start to sing, a choir of many, many voices, and for a brief moment she thought she heard her own voice singing with them:

> *I cannot find my way.*
> *I cannot find my way.*

I cannot find my way at all.
There are so many choices,
So many different voices.
I cannot find my way at all.

John ceremoniously took the large star out of the suit-case of ornaments. Constance had never before seen a Christmas ornament so beautiful, and his forgotten carol told the story behind the star:

There were three kings who followed the star of Bethlehem.
They came from afar to praise and honor Him.
The light which beckoned
Them to seek the Lord of men:
It calls to you,
It calls to me.

The sound of the choir again returned, only fuller this time, as if more voices had joined:

We cannot find our way.
We cannot find our way.
We cannot find our way at all.
There are so many choices,
So many different voices.
We cannot find our way at all.

As if to answer all the voices, John sang more surely
and more powerfully than he ever had before:

> We're not alone;
> We have a star that shines today.
> The love He gave teaches how
> And shows the way.
> The light is clear to see
> If we have faith and believe.
> Three kings found the Lord,
> And so can we.

The choir sang counter to John:

> We cannot find our way.
> We cannot find our way at all.

But John confidently repeated his claim:

> Three kings found the Lord, and so can we.
> And if you've lost your way,
> That light burns bright today.
> And it will shine eternally.
>
> Three kings found the Lord,
> And so can we.
> Three kings found the Lord,
> And so can we.

> *Three kings found the Lord,*
> *And so must we.*

The message of John's forgotten carol overwhelmed the voices of despair and confusion, and the choir began to sing,

> *Lord, help us find our way.*
> *We need to find our way.*
> *Lord, help us find our way back home.*

As it did, Constance heard her voice joining in, and for the first time since her dance the night before, she felt harmony in her soul. So when John invited Constance to place the star at the top of the tree, she agreed willingly.

To reach the top, she would need a stepladder, so John went to get one for her. While he was gone, she got a chance to study the star more carefully. She noticed a pearl in its very center, framed by four indentations. Three of those were filled with what looked like a ruby, an emerald, and a sapphire. The fourth indentation was empty. When John returned with the ladder, he explained that the pearl at the center represented the Lord, and the three gems represented the three kings who sought Him, found

Him, and honored Him. The empty space, he told her, was for all of us who needed to follow their example.

John then steadied the ladder as Constance placed the crowning ornament on the tree. She wanted it to be perfect, so she asked John to step back a few feet and let her know if it looked straight. When a knock came at the front door, John excused himself to answer it. Constance wondered where the butler was when they needed him.

From her vantage point on the ladder, she couldn't clearly see or hear everything that was happening in the entry, but what she did hear frightened her. She caught little pieces of phrases: "You'll have to come with us." . . . "Did you really think you could get away with this again?" . . . "You have the right to remain silent . . ."

Constance went numb for a moment, frozen on the ladder. She didn't know what to do. After a moment or two, a policeman entered the living room and saw Constance on the stepladder looking a bit like a kitten caught in a tree.

"You must be the nurse from the hospital," he said a bit gruffly.

"What are you doing here? What's going on, officer?" she called down to him.

"The neighbors called us because they knew the family was on vacation in Europe and were concerned that strangers were in the house."

"But this is his house! He's their uncle, and I'm here at their request, caring for him."

"I've got to hand it to the man. He's clever. But he's done this before and kind of gave himself away this time. Don't you want to get down from there?" he asked, and Constance obeyed.

"What do you mean he's done this before, officer?"

"A couple of years ago in Granville, a lonely old man sent a wire to a nearby hospital saying that if they would send a nurse to care for the family's aging uncle while they were in Europe, there was a good chance they'd get some kind of donation when they returned."

Constance turned as white as the snow outside. "What happened?" she asked.

"Well, from what the Granville sheriff told us, he

didn't hurt anybody or steal anything. In fact, the crazy old coot even gave some money to the hospital."

"So why did he do it?"

"Huh! Who knows? Maybe he didn't want to spend Christmas alone." The officer shook his head. "Look, I'll need you to come down to the station with me for some routine questioning, and then we'll let you go. Sorry for the inconvenience."

"What's going to happen to him?" she asked.

"He's probably homeless or senile. We'll let him spend a night or two at the jail until we can find out if he's got any relatives. Then, if no charges are pressed against him, we'll try to find an institution that will take him."

Constance gathered her things and rode to the county jail with the officer. He talked on his police radio most of the ride, but Constance didn't hear much of what he was saying; she was lost in a world of her own. At first she was in shock. Then she tried to put the pieces together. And then she became angry—angry at John for playing such a cruel practical joke on her. Maybe it wasn't meant to be a joke on her, but it was. She felt used, deceived, taken advantage of. And the more she thought about it, the angrier she became.

After arriving at the station and answering a few questions and giving her statement, she asked if she could see John before she left. She didn't tell the officer why, but she wanted to give him a piece of her mind. While she waited to see if a final meeting with her "patient" could be arranged, she called the hospital, trying to get through to Mr. Halifax, but he could not be reached. She decided that any message she might leave would only confuse him, since she was still confused herself, so she said she'd talk to him in the morning.

It took some doing, but the officer arranged for her to have a few minutes with John before taking him away. "Would you like to have me there as a protection?" he asked her.

"For me or for him?" she asked, and she saw a sly grin come over the officer's face.

"Well, you both look pretty harmless to me. But in case you have a problem, just holler. I'll be right outside the room."

She entered the cubicle where John was sitting and stood in front of him. She wasn't planning on sitting down. She was going to tell him a thing or two and then make a dramatic exit. Since she hadn't had time to really plan what she was going to say or do, she had no idea what would happen. But she didn't care about any of that. She just wanted to let the volcano that was bubbling inside her erupt.

"Well, Mr. *Truth*, this must be a little awkward for you," she began. "Just when you had me right where you wanted me, someone pulled back the curtain, and there you stood, like the mighty Wizard of Oz, revealed as the fraud and scam artist you are. Tell me, is it exciting to play with someone's heart and mind? Does it give you a feeling of power?"

John sat listening, quietly and somehow understandingly. "I wasn't playing."

"You *weren't?* Then *what did you think you were doing?*" Constance was stunned to hear herself shout at the old man. It frightened her because she didn't know what else would come out, and she couldn't stop it.

"You took advantage of me. I don't know how, but you knew my weaknesses, my vulnerabilities. Just like my mother, you manipulated my emotions, as a sculptor molds his clay. Only you made me something I didn't want to be." As the words flowed out, so did her tears. "You made me something I didn't want to be! *And then you left me—you lied to me and then you left!*" She was sobbing inconsolably. "I *hate* you for hurting me . . ."

John reached out to comfort her. "Don't touch me, Mother. . . . I'm furious with you . . ." Her words lingered in the air and mingled with the sound of her crying. A flood of hurt poured out and then buried itself in John's shoulder. As she wept, he gently stroked her hair and whispered, "Let it all out, Connie Lou. Let it all out."

As much as she hurt, she was beginning to feel cleansed somehow, as if she were washing out an infection in the deepest part of her soul. When the reservoir of tears was empty and she began to breathe normally, John held her by the shoulders and made her look at him.

"You can start to heal now, Connie Lou," he said tenderly.

CHAPTER 9

The Carol in Her Heart

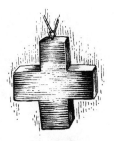

The guard came in to take John away. Constance wanted a few more minutes, but she couldn't have them. John asked her for a favor. "Could you get my ornaments for me . . . please?" he said, and then he was gone.

Constance didn't know if she could do what he asked her. She didn't know if the ornaments were some sort of evidence she wasn't supposed to touch, so she asked the officer if it was all right to return to the house and collect the ornaments along with the rest of his things. He smiled and said he'd arrange for someone to take her.

On the ride back to the mansion, Constance planned what she would do. She'd first check to see if John's clothes, his flute, and the shepherd's costume were upstairs in his room. Then she'd get his ornament case, place it near the tree, and then put the ornaments all back in the antique suitcase that carried them. By the time she'd made these plans and had a few mental reviews for possible problems, the police car pulled into the mansion's driveway.

Returning to the house knowing that John wouldn't be there was odd. She wondered if the butler would be bumbling around somewhere. Immediately upon entering, she set out to execute her plan, first going upstairs to see if anything was left in John's room, wherever that was. At the top of the stairs she saw a hall with several doors, but since only one was open, she thought she'd try there first.

On the bed were some things she expected to see—

and a few she didn't. John's sweater was there. And his shepherd's clothing. And his flute. But next to the flute was a wig and a beard, thick glasses, some padding, and the clothes she had seen the butler wear—in those few glimpses she'd had of him. She was surprised, but then again, she wasn't that surprised the more she thought about it.

Her greatest surprise came when she went downstairs and collected the old Christmas ornament suitcase. When she picked it up to move it closer to the tree, a flap inside the lid fell open, and out spilled several newspaper articles and an envelope. In the envelope was a cashier's check made out to the Fullerton Hospital for five thousand dollars. Not exactly a major endowment, but it was a promised gift nonetheless. Constance wondered where a man like John could have come up with the money. She hoped it wasn't stolen.

The newspaper articles were in various shades of aging yellow, but the headlines carried similar themes. One article from the *Granville Gazette* in December of 1988 was cleverly headlined:

DECK THE HALLS WITH BOWS OF FOLLY

It appears that Santa isn't the only one who sneaks into people's houses to surprise them at Christmastime. Last week, in the suburb of . . .

The article went on to explain what the officer had told her—that John "borrowed" the homes of wealthy people who were away during the holidays and then arranged for a nurse to spend the holiday "caring" for him in exchange for a promised but undisclosed gift. Constance didn't like the article because the tone was too facetious. She picked up another. This one, dated December 27, 1974, came from a small-town paper in Missouri:

BUTCHER CLAIMS CON MAN
TAUGHT HIM FORGOTTEN CAROLS

A local butcher claims that a mysterious customer taught him Christmas carols about forgotten parts of the Christian holiday . . .

Though the article wasn't about a nurse, Constance

recognized unmistakable similarities to what had happened to her.

She read article after article in newspapers from all across North America. Uncle John had really been around. *He must have been fairly young when he started doing this*, she thought when she read the article from the *Des Moines Register* of December 1948. But then she noticed that he was referred to as a "dignified but aging gentleman suffering from a mild psychosis."

There were several articles from the War years and the Depression, and they all told the same basic story, yet the tone of the articles during those difficult years was different, like the headline from a New York newspaper in the 1940s:

NEW YORK FAMILY CLAIMS THEIR OWN MIRACLE ON 34th ST.

The farther back Constance read, the more fragile was the paper of the articles, and the darker their color. She felt compelled to read every one. But as the dates on the papers approached the turn of the century, she got chills. And then she saw something that changed everything.

It wasn't a particularly different headline from all the rest, and the story was certainly familiar enough—but the date on the paper it was taken from was December 29, 1805.

Constance carefully returned the articles to their special compartment in the suitcase and reported to the officer, who was on the phone in the other room, about the cashier's check to the hospital. Then she proceeded to take the ornaments off the tree. As she held each one, she was enveloped in the memories and the melodies that accompanied them. She rediscovered the significance and meaning of each one: the star; the cradle; the bow made of swaddling clothes; the corsage of dried flowers; the composer's pen; the shepherd's flute; the entrance to the inn. All filled her heart again as she placed them in their appointed place in the leather and wood case.

There wasn't a place for the newest ornament in the collection—the red cross. And no melody came quickly to her mind as she held it. But one was there, buried in her heart, and without her knowing how it happened, suddenly it was set free.

I thought I'd seen all the lights and sung all the songs.
I felt the holiday lasted a bit too long.
I never shed any tears
When Christmas was through,
Until I celebrated one with you. And now
I cry the day that I take the tree down.
I want the season to last all year round.
When I'm surrounded by these memories,
It's almost like you're here with me.

As she sang, she also danced with a partner who wasn't there. Had anyone been watching, they'd have noticed that every gesture, every glance, every movement made it clear that whoever she was remembering was someone very special.

It's strange how things are changed
When touched by love.
We treasure things we never thought much of.

I cry the day that I take the tree down.
And I want the season to last all year round.
And I am dreaming of Christmases when
We'll be together again.

She could hardly finish the song for the tears. She'd

never cried tears like that before. They were cleansing tears that carried a lifetime of unexpressed feelings. They were tears of love lost and love found. They were tears of understanding of all she had missed, and tears of gratitude for all she could now receive. When she had cried them all out, she felt reborn.

Oh, how she wished that John could have heard her carol—the one he had told her she was writing in her heart. Of all the people in the world, he was the one she most wanted to share it with. Perhaps she would have that chance when she returned his ornaments, she thought.

Not knowing whether to keep her red cross or to place it in the case, she decided at length to place it with the other ornaments. She felt that it would be a unique honor to have something of herself in such company.

CHAPTER 10

In His Love There Is a Home

When Constance returned to the jail, she asked if she might see John one last time and give him his treasured Christmas ornaments. They said she couldn't, because he was gone.

Gone? she thought. *How could he be gone?* The policeman said that someone who claimed to be like family to him came and got him out. He thought her name might have been Sarah, but he couldn't remember.

"But he left this for you," the policeman said as he handed her an envelope that Constance quietly opened and read in the hallway that led to the jail.

My Dearest Connie Lou,

Thanks so much for everything. You'll never know how much knowing you has enriched my life. I want you to have the ornaments as my Christmas present to you. After so many years of traveling, I feel they need a permanent home . . .

While she was reading, she was distracted by the sound of singing down the hall, and the tune was hauntingly familiar. It sounded as though it might be coming from one of the jail cells. When she focused on the singing long enough to understand the words, she recognized it as the Christmas carol she'd heard before by a group of singers huddled around a fire that was burning in a garbage can painted like a Christmas tree:

Homeless, homeless,
Like the Christ child was . . . we are
Homeless, homeless,
But there is hope because . . .

It was one of John's forgotten carols. He'd taught it to give hope and dignity to the homeless living on the streets, and now, in just a few hours in the jail, John had shared it again with others who needed to be lifted.

Just sitting in the hallway listening to the forgotten carol made her feel close to him. She turned to the final words of his letter:

I too am dreaming of Christmases when we'll be together again.

Merry Christmas,
John

He *had* heard her song, *her* forgotten carol. He had heard it long before she knew it had been written. She tenderly held the note and pressed it against her heart. She rocked back and forth and found herself singing the carol with the homeless carolers in the county jail—not with sadness or loneliness or despair but with dignity and hope. And as she sang, she no longer wondered where those feelings came from. She knew.

As she tried to imagine how she would describe John to others when she told her story, the only word that came instantly to mind was *beloved.*

The next morning, Constance got a chance to tell Mr. Halifax what had happened, and she presented him with the check for five thousand dollars. She prevented him from acting disappointed with the amount by spouting the virtues he himself had espoused at every telethon he'd ever appeared on in behalf of the hospital: "Your contribution, even a few dollars," she half impersonated his delivery, "will be a living, working legacy here at Fullerton Hospital." She silently dared him to say anything after that.

Then she informed him that she'd like to work Christmas day and give some of the nurses a chance to be with their families. She surprised him again when she asked if she could help in the maternity ward. She made sure she was scheduled, and then she left his office.

On Christmas day, there were three glorious miracles

at Fullerton Hospital. Three new babies came into the world, and Constance was there for all three. During one of her breaks, she just watched the new fathers and mothers marvel at their newborn children. One of the fathers recognized the nurse who had helped with the delivery of his son and approached her.

"You were there, weren't you? Thanks for being with us when you probably wanted to be home with your family. I'm just so grateful for everything, and I wanted to wish you a Merry Christmas, Ms. . . . Ms. . . ." He struggled to see her name tag, but it was covered by a blanket she had over her shoulder.

"My name is Constance," she said almost automatically. But she paused. And as she looked into the eyes of the young father, his sweetness reminded her of a dear friend. And she smiled. "But my friends call me Connie Lou."